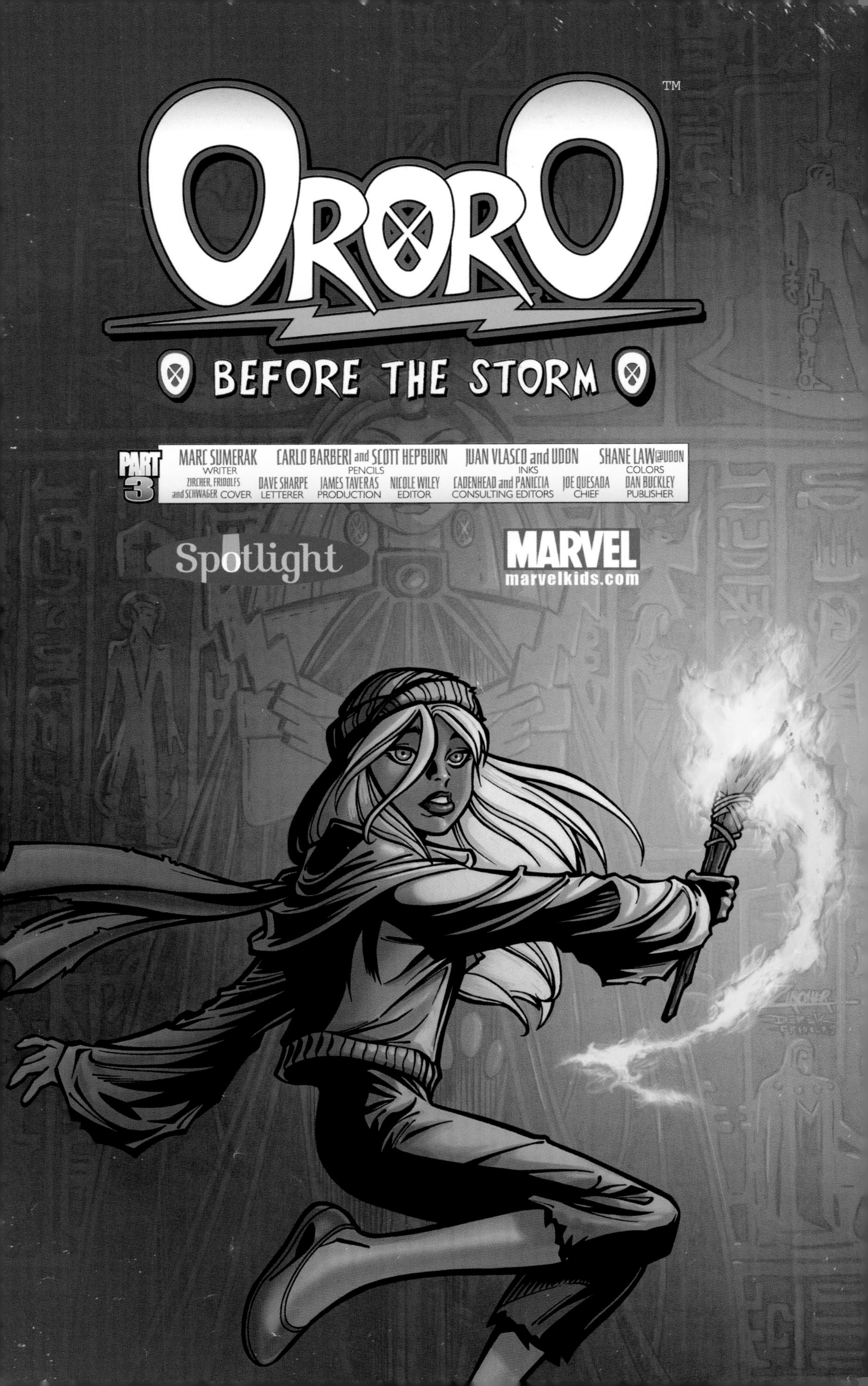
ORORO™
BEFORE THE STORM
PART 3
MARC SUMERAK WRITER
CARLO BARBERI and SCOTT HEPBURN PENCILS
JUAN VLASCO and UDON INKS
SHANE LAW@UDON COLORS
ZIRCHER, FRIDOLFS and SCHWAGER COVER
DAVE SHARPE LETTERER
JAMES TAVERAS PRODUCTION
NICOLE WILEY EDITOR
CADENHEAD and PANICCIA CONSULTING EDITORS
JOE QUESADA CHIEF
DAN BUCKLEY PUBLISHER
Spotlight
MARVEL
marvelkids.com

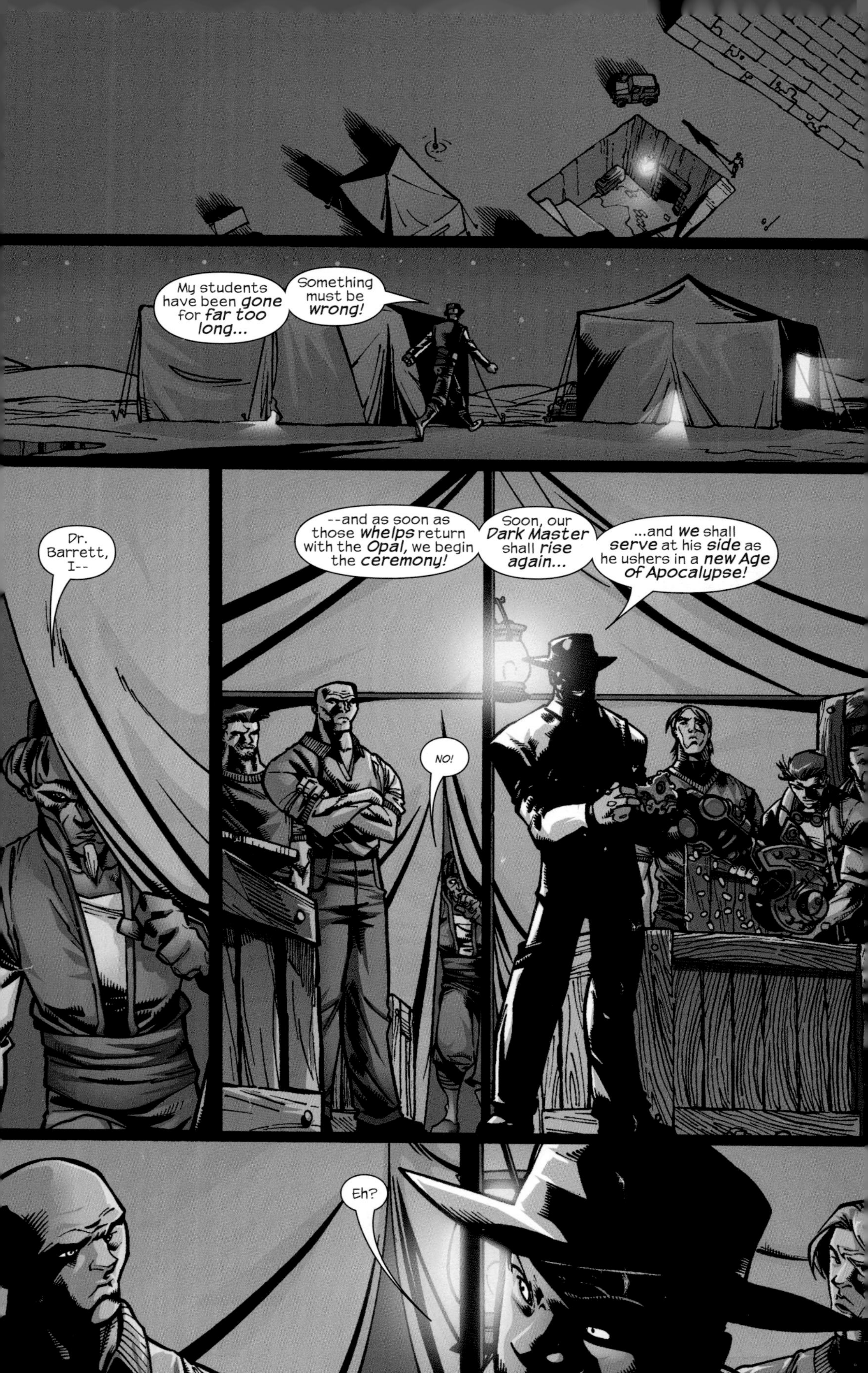
My students have been gone for far too long...
Something must be wrong!
Dr. Barrett, I--
--and as soon as those whelps return with the Opal, we begin the ceremony!
Soon, our Dark Master shall rise again...
...and we shall serve at his side as he ushers in a new Age of Apocalypse!
NO!
Eh?

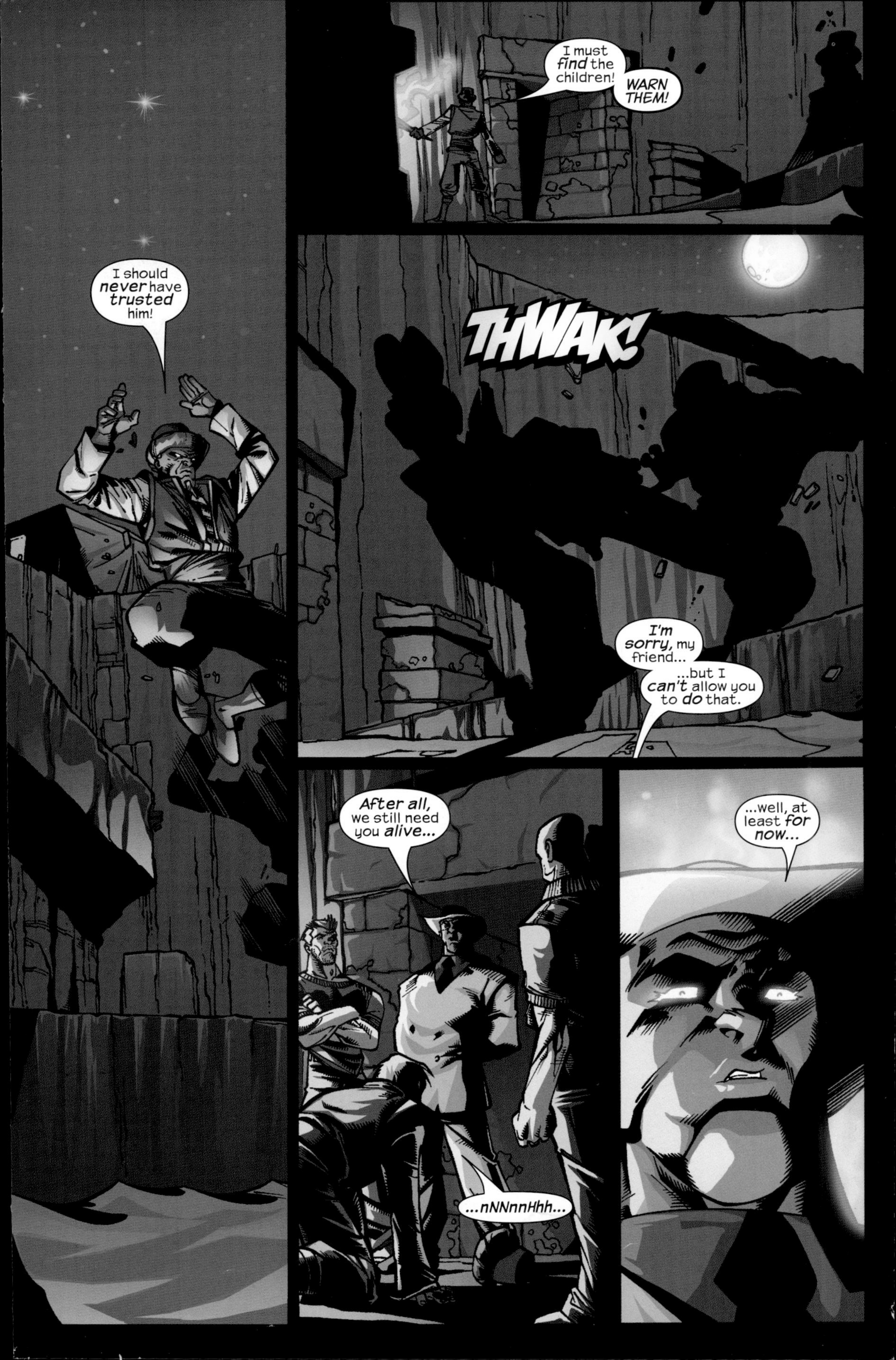
I should never have trusted him!
I must find the children!
WARN THEM!
THWAK!
I'm sorry, my friend...
...but I can't allow you to do that.
After all, we still need you alive...
...nNNnnHhh...
...well, at least for now...

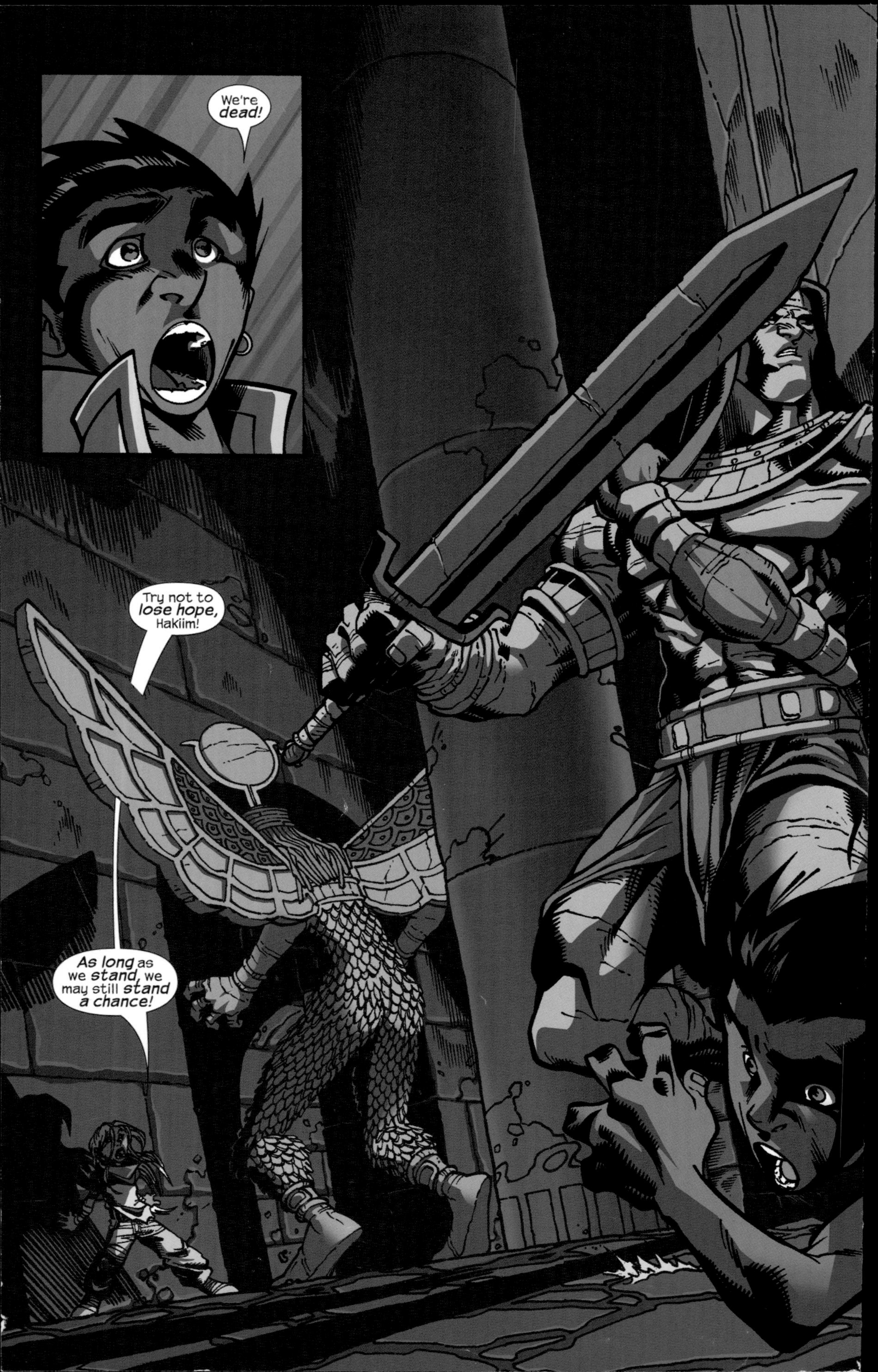
We're dead!
Try not to lose hope, Hakiim!
As long as we stand, we may still stand a chance!

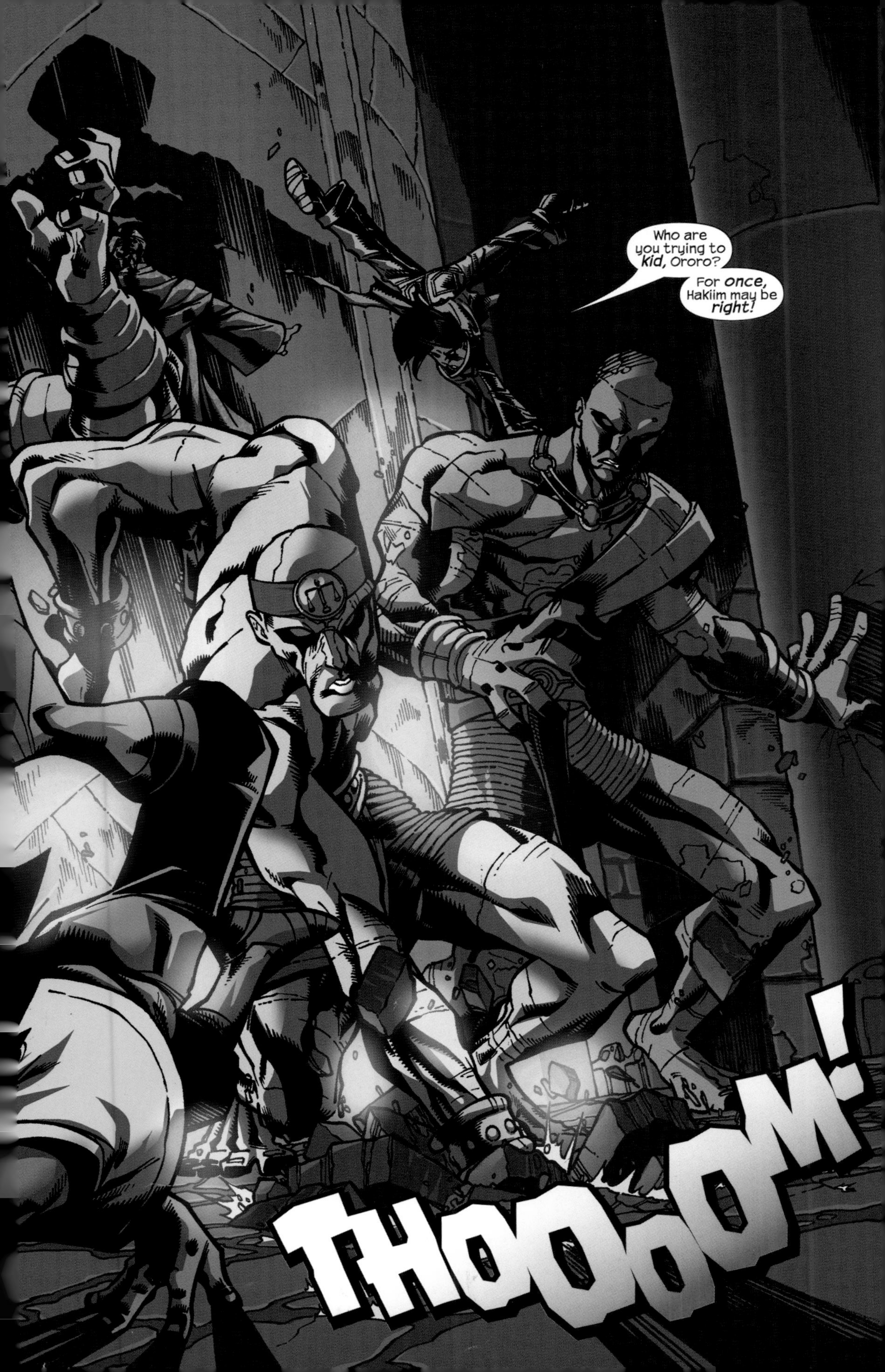
Who are you trying to kid, Ororo?
For once, Hakiim may be right!
THOOOOM!

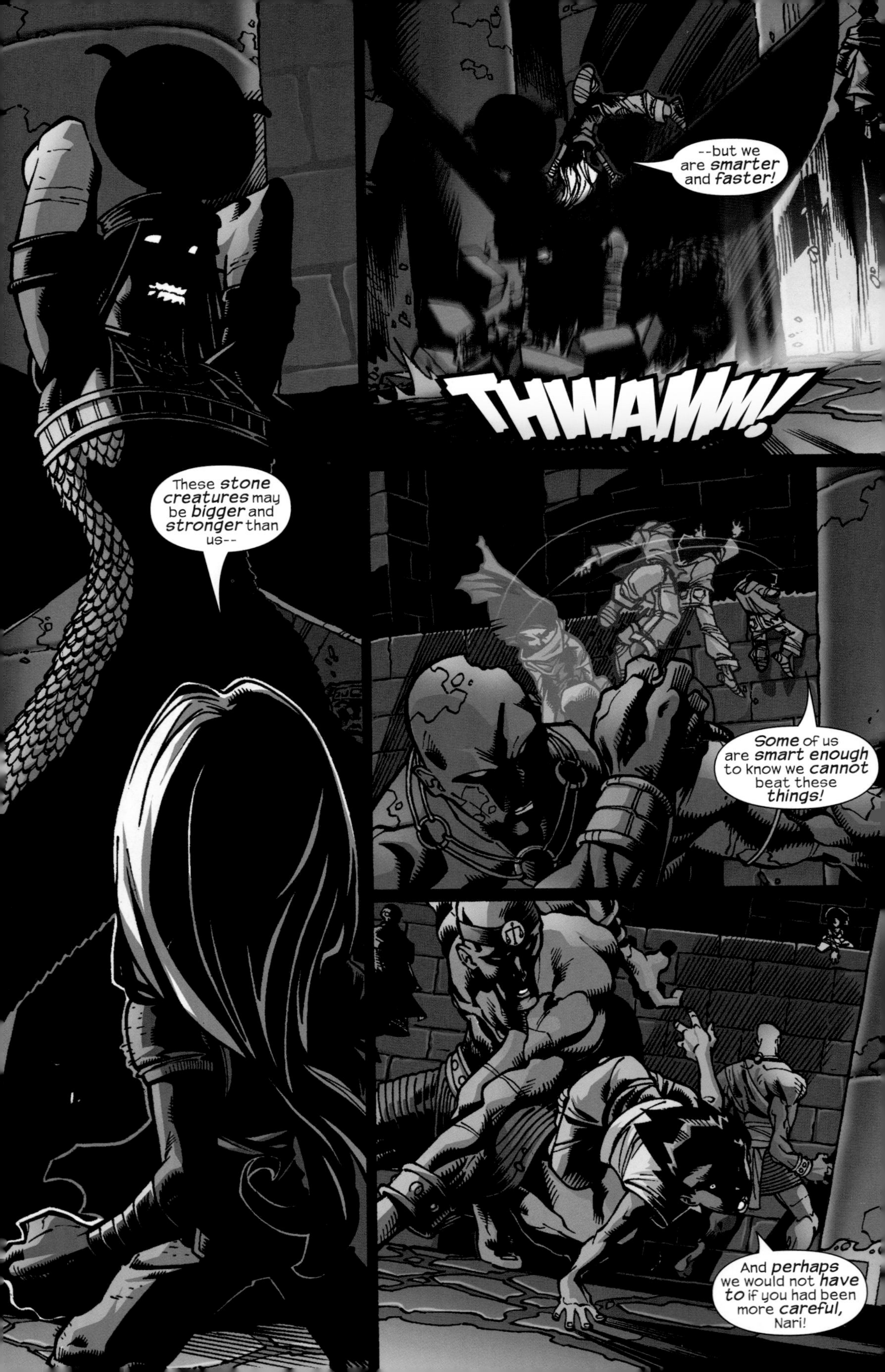
These stone creatures may be bigger and stronger than us--
--but we are smarter and faster!
THWAMM!
Some of us are smart enough to know we cannot beat these things!
And perhaps we would not have to if you had been more careful, Nari!

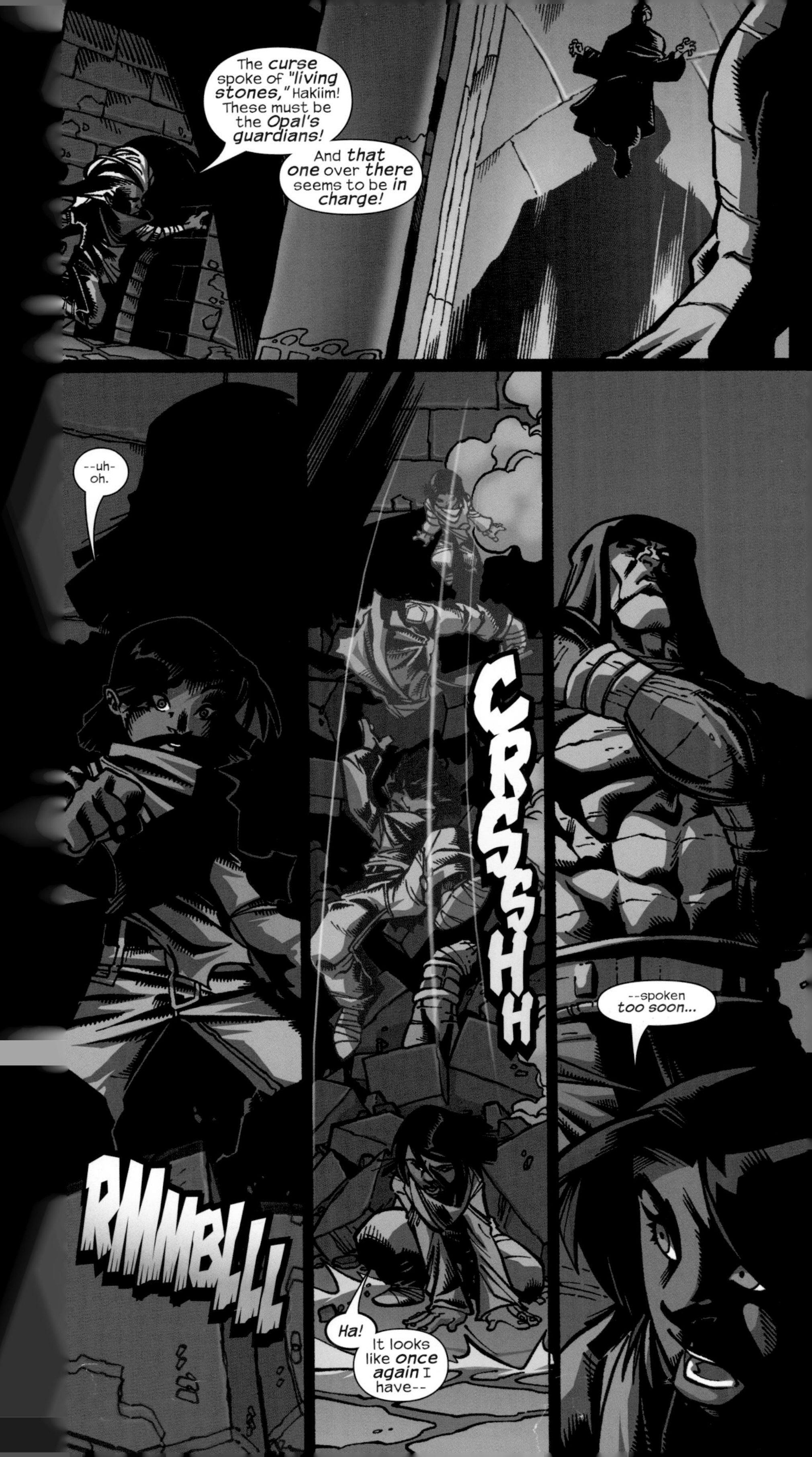
The curse spoke of "living stones," Hakiim! These must be the Opal's guardians!
And that one over there seems to be in charge!
--uh-oh.
RMMBLLL
CRSSHH
Ha!
It looks like once again I have--
--spoken too soon...

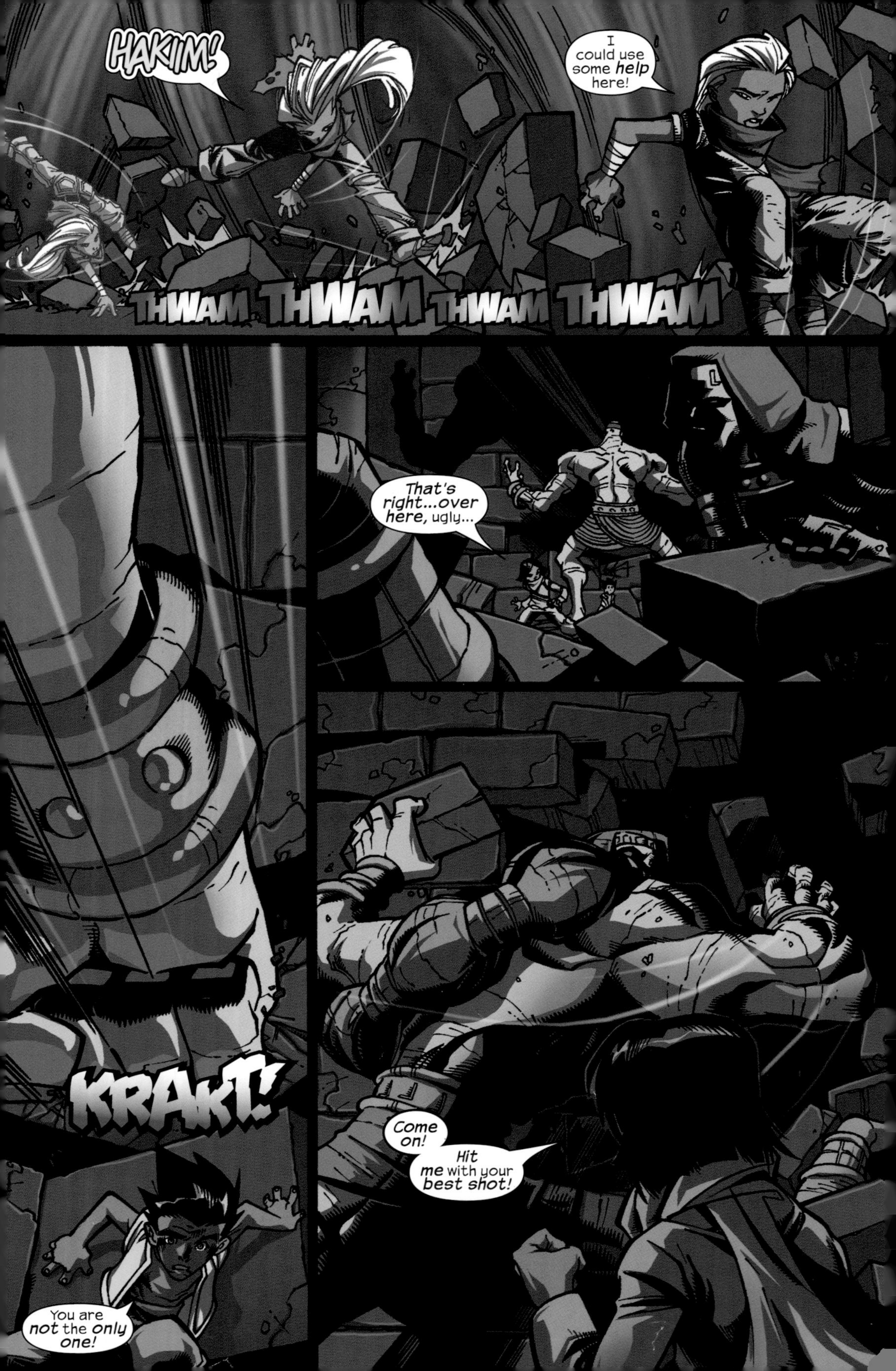
HAKIIM!
I could use some help here!
THWAM THWAM THWAM THWAM
KRAKT!
That's right...over here, ugly...
Come on!
Hit me with your best shot!
You are not the only one!

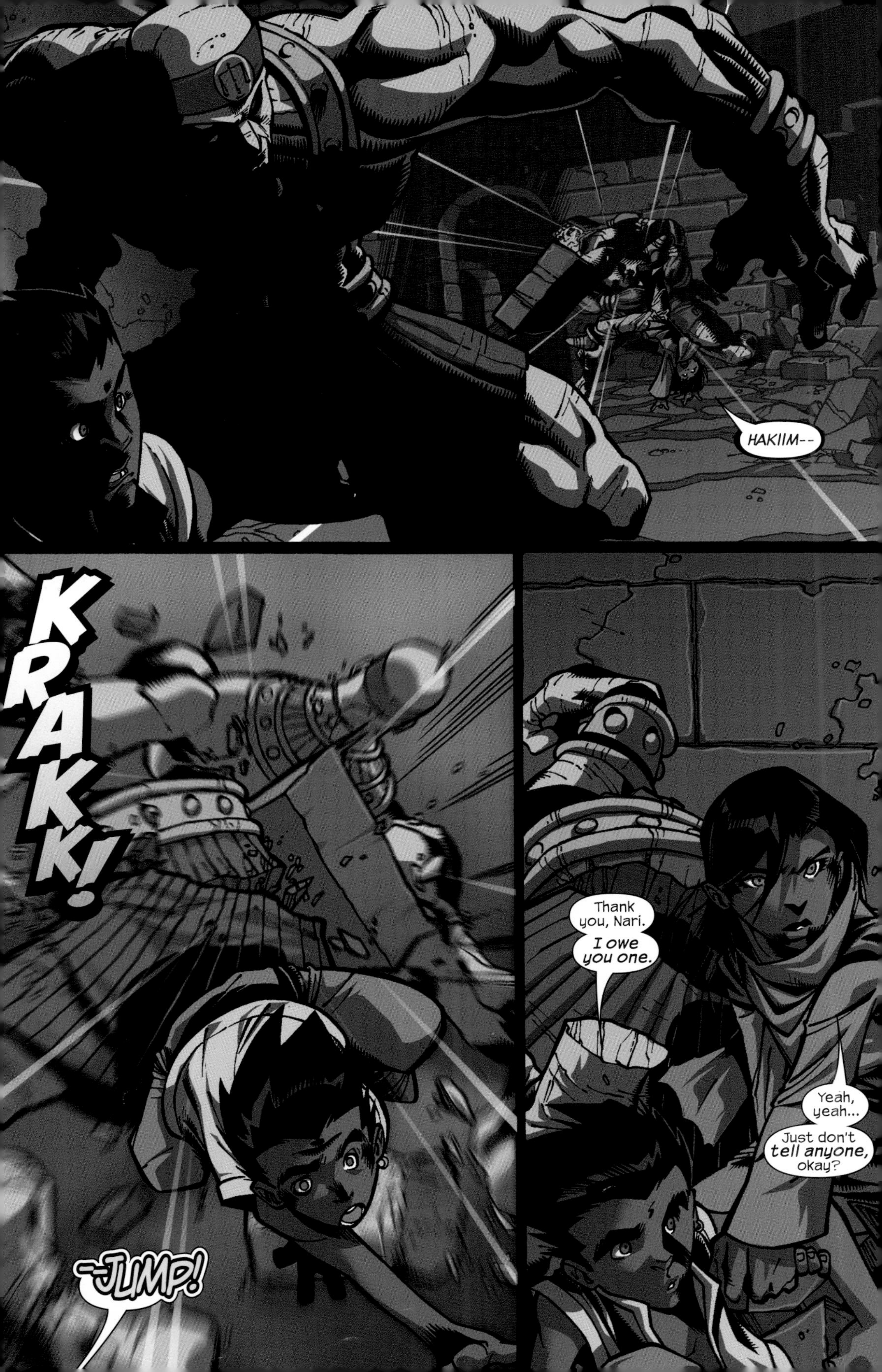
HAKIIM--
KRAKK!
--JUMP!
Thank you, Nari. I owe you one.
Yeah, yeah... Just don't tell anyone, okay?

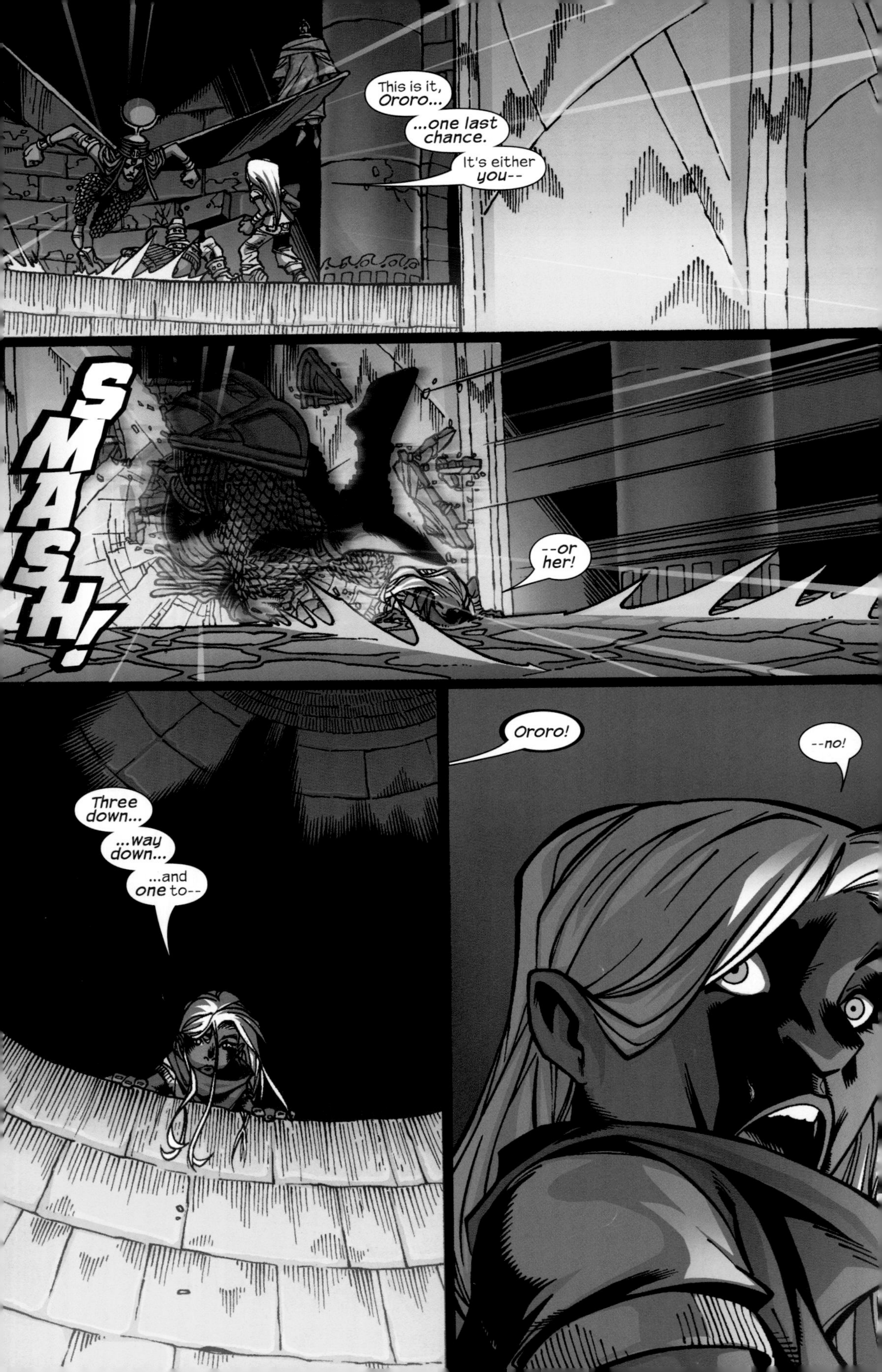
This is it, Ororo...
...one last chance.
It's either you--
SMASH!
--or her!
Three down...
...way down...
...and one to--
Ororo!
--no!

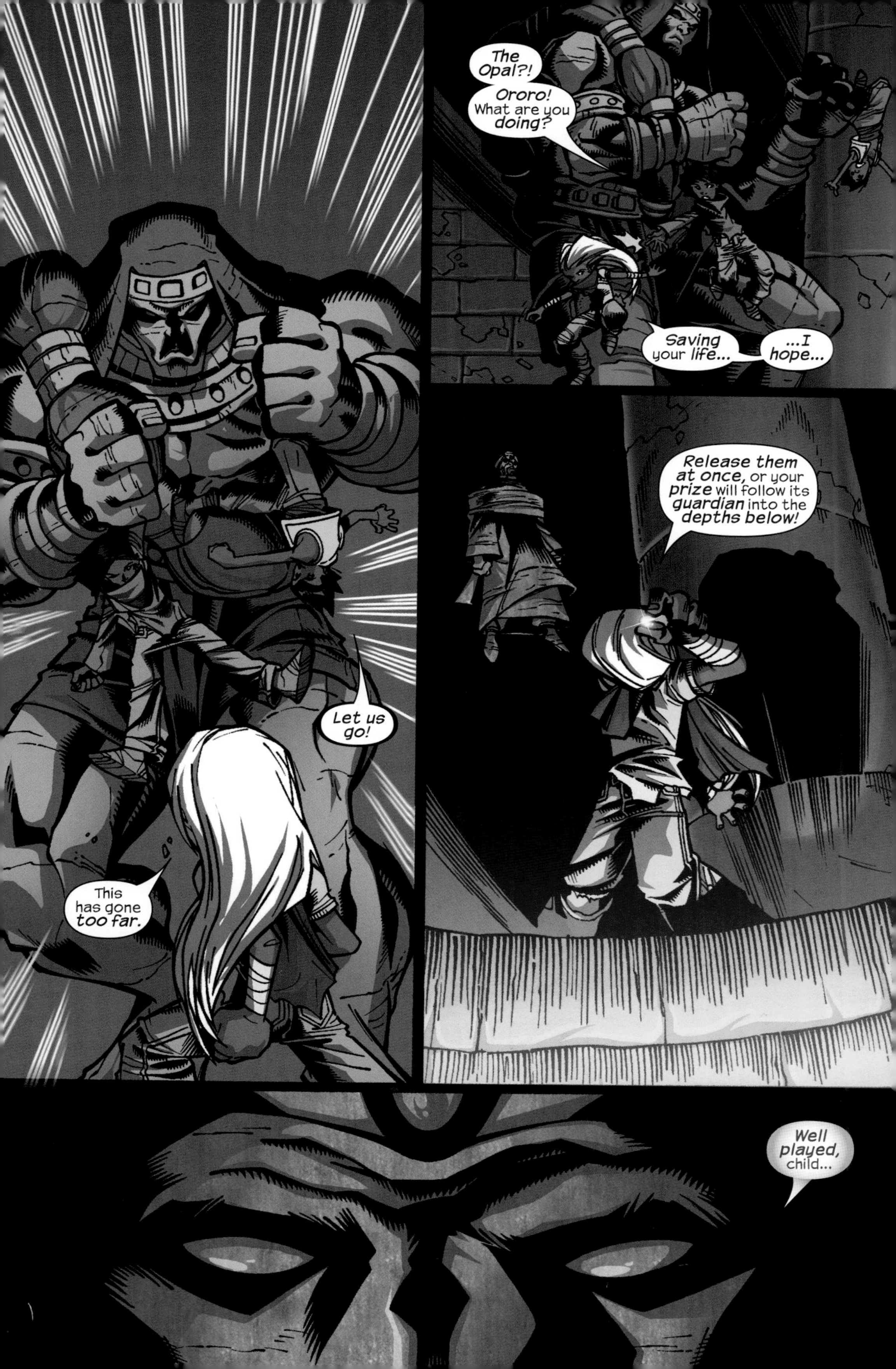
This has gone too far.
Let us go!
The Opal?!
Ororo! What are you doing?
Saving your life...
...I hope...
Release them at once, or your prize will follow its guardian into the depths below!
Well played, child...

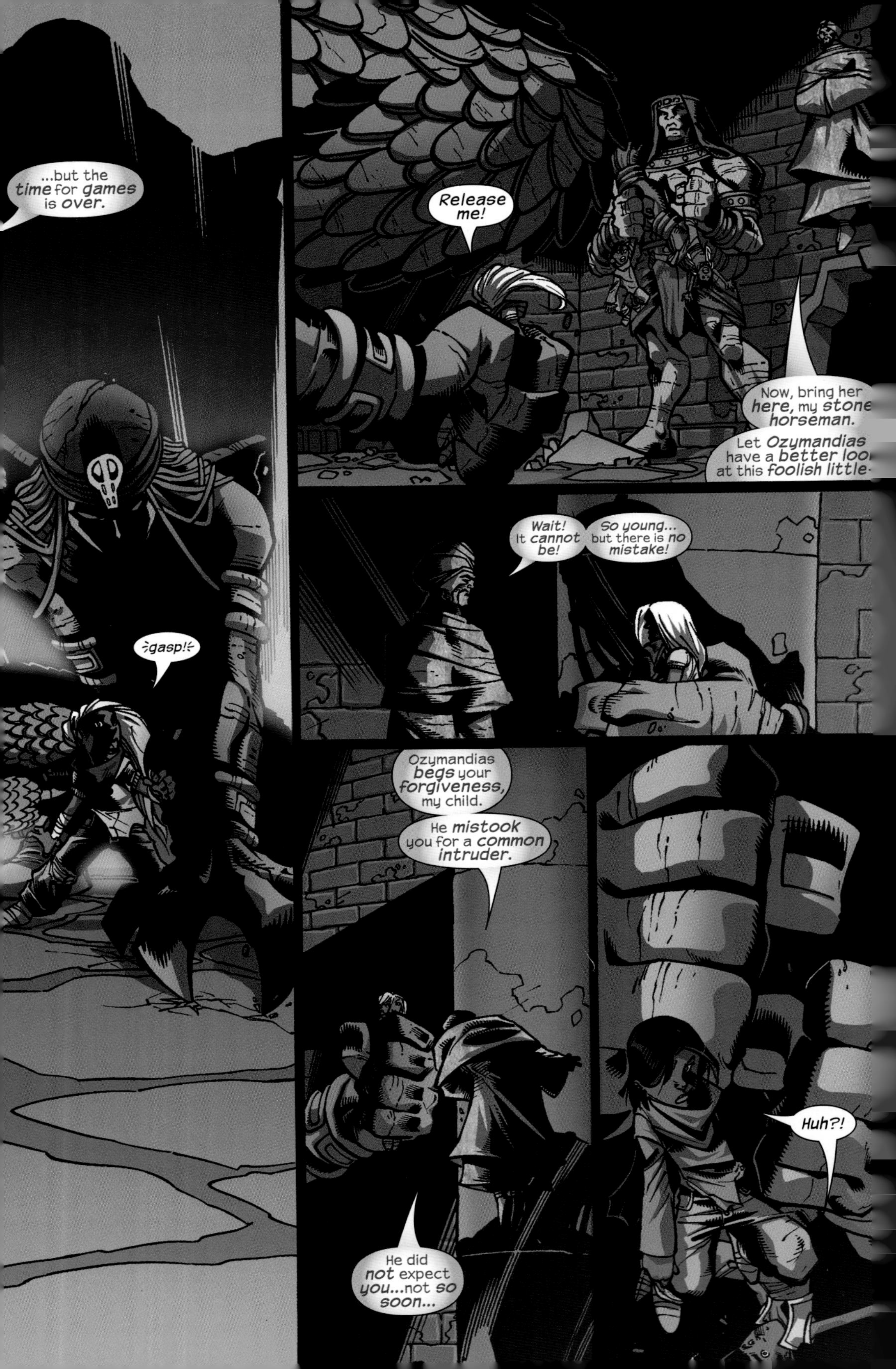
...but the time for games is over.
Release me!
Now, bring her here, my stone horseman.
Let Ozymandias have a better loo at this foolish little-
-gasp!-
Wait! It cannot be!
So young... but there is no mistake!
Ozymandias begs your forgiveness, my child.
He mistook you for a common intruder.
He did not expect you...not so soon...
Huh?!

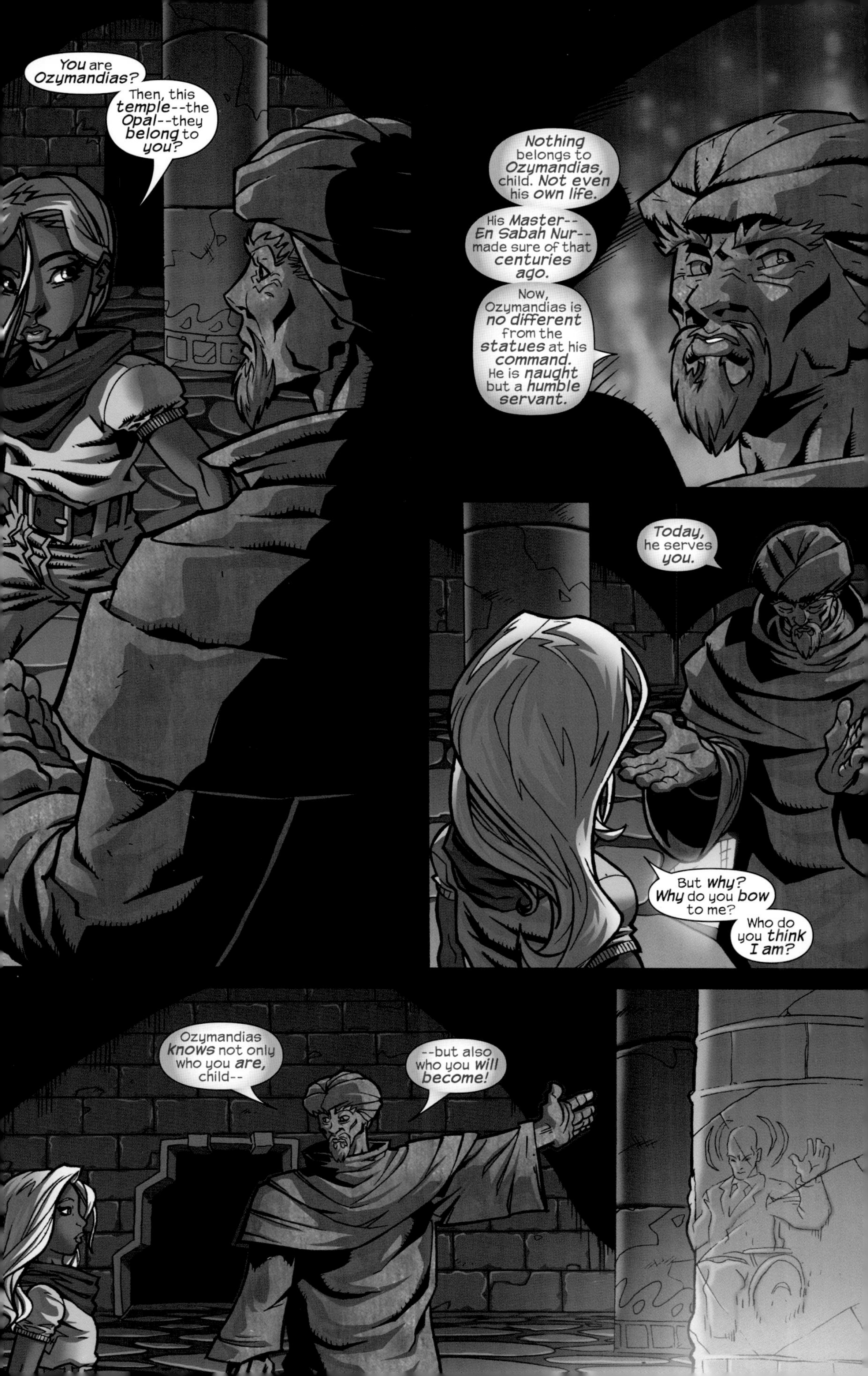
You are Ozymandias?
Then, this temple--the Opal--they belong to you?
Nothing belongs to Ozymandias, child. Not even his own life.
His Master--En Sabah Nur--made sure of that centuries ago.
Now, Ozymandias is no different from the statues at his command. He is naught but a humble servant.
Today, he serves you.
But why? Why do you bow to me?
Who do you think I am?
Ozymandias knows not only who you are, child--
--but also who you will become!

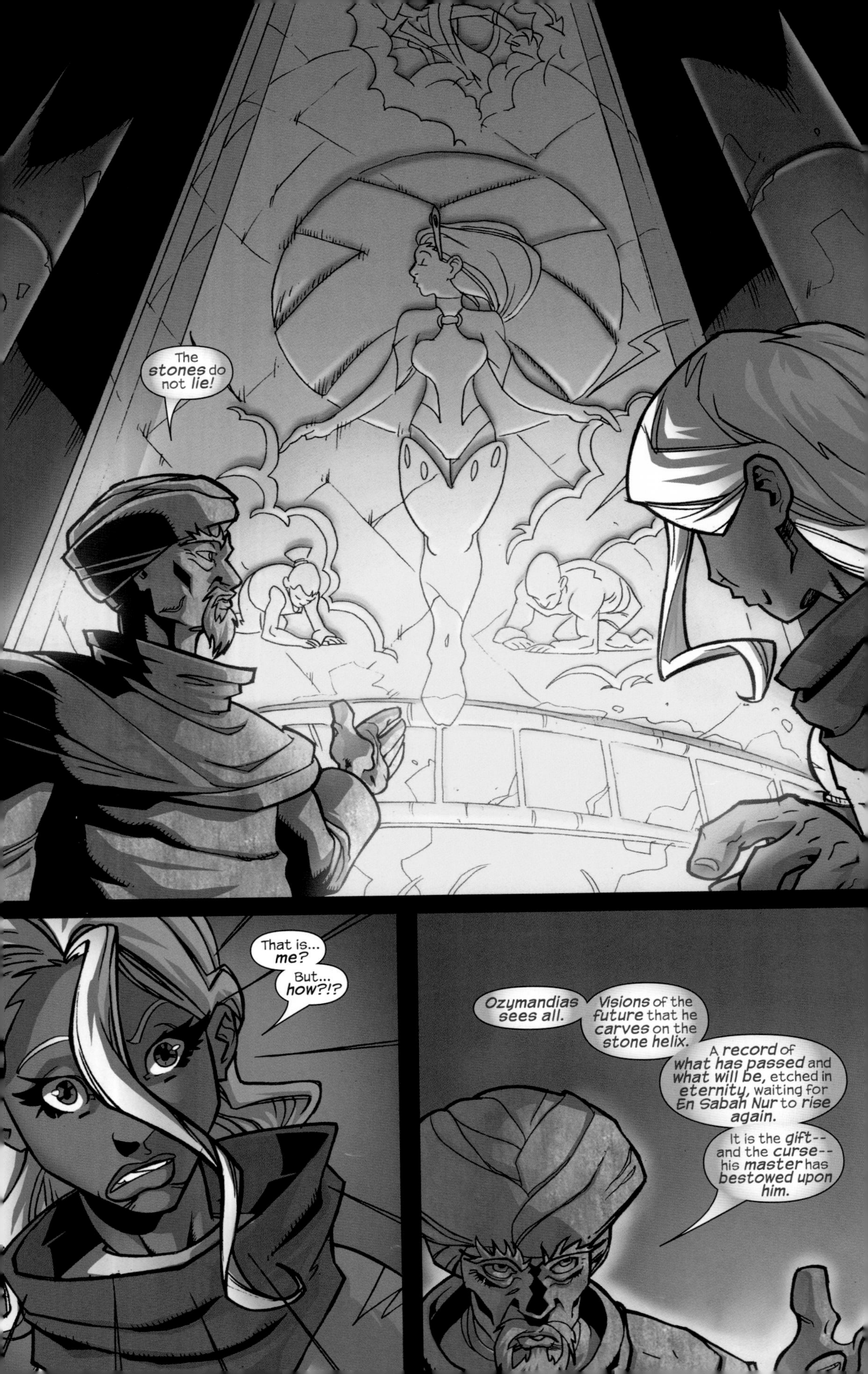
The stones do not lie!
That is... me?
But... how?!?
Ozymandias sees all.
Visions of the future that he carves on the stone helix.
A record of what has passed and what will be, etched in eternity, waiting for En Sabah Nur to rise again.
It is the gift-- and the curse-- his master has bestowed upon him.

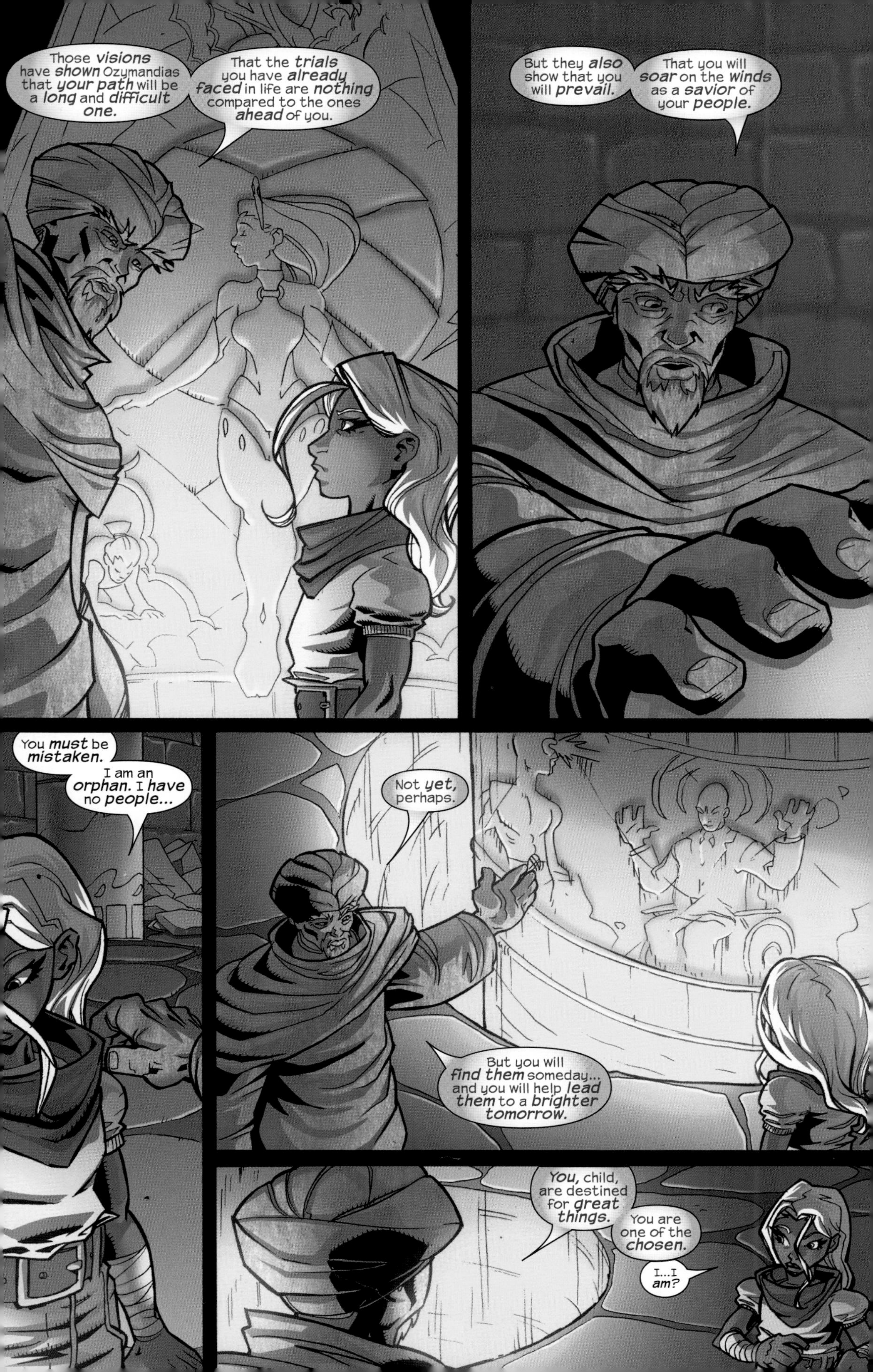
Those visions have shown Ozymandias that your path will be a long and difficult one.
That the trials you have already faced in life are nothing compared to the ones ahead of you.
But they also show that you will prevail.
That you will soar on the winds as a savior of your people.
You must be mistaken.
I am an orphan. I have no people...
Not yet, perhaps.
But you will find them someday... and you will help lead them to a brighter tomorrow.
You, child, are destined for great things.
You are one of the chosen.
I...I am?

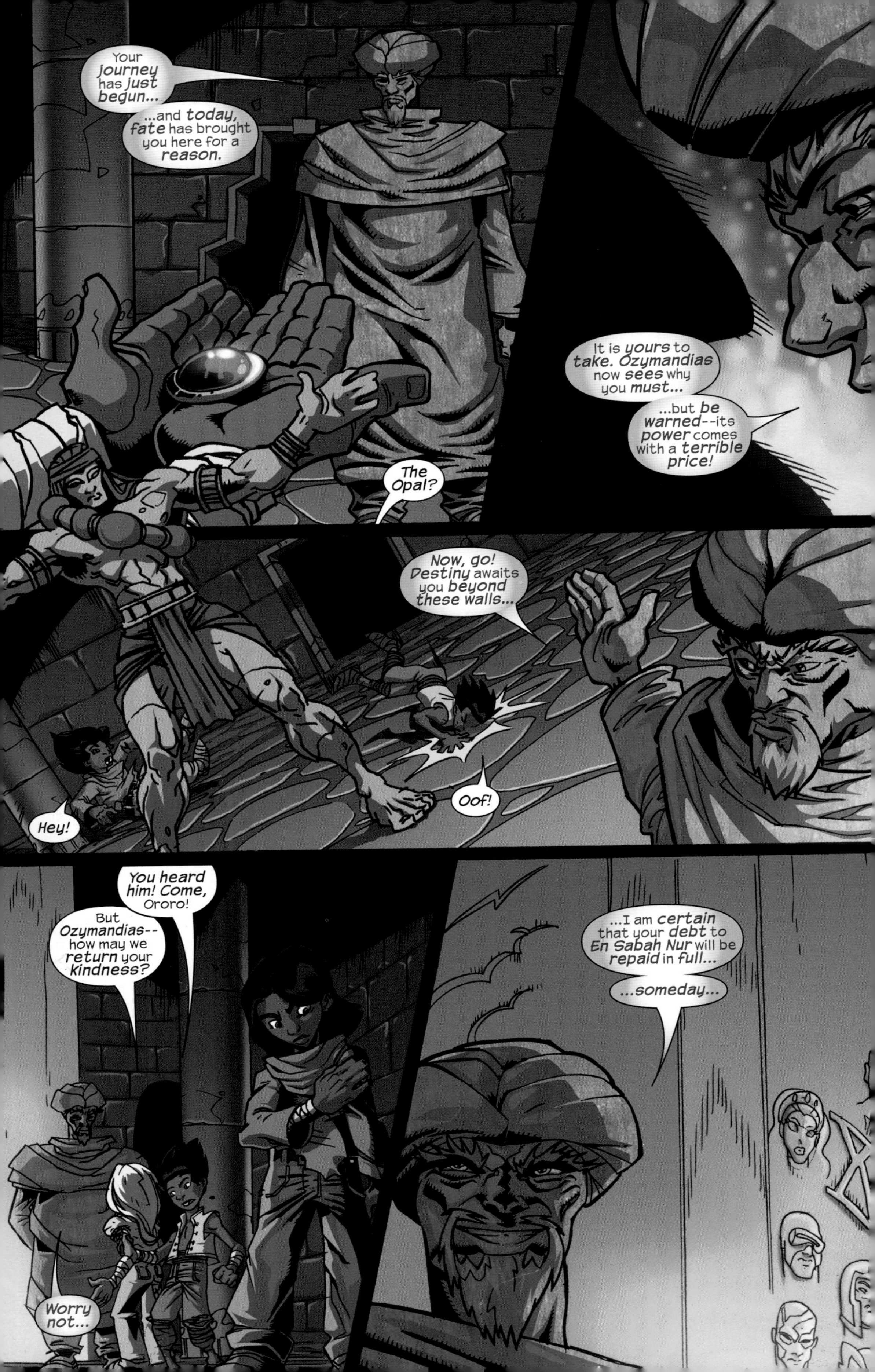
Your journey has just begun...
...and today, fate has brought you here for a reason.
The Opal?
It is yours to take. Ozymandias now sees why you must...
...but be warned--its power comes with a terrible price!
Now, go! Destiny awaits you beyond these walls...
Hey!
Oof!
You heard him! Come, Ororo!
But Ozymandias--how may we return your kindness?
Worry not...
...I am certain that your debt to En Sabah Nur will be repaid in full...
...someday...

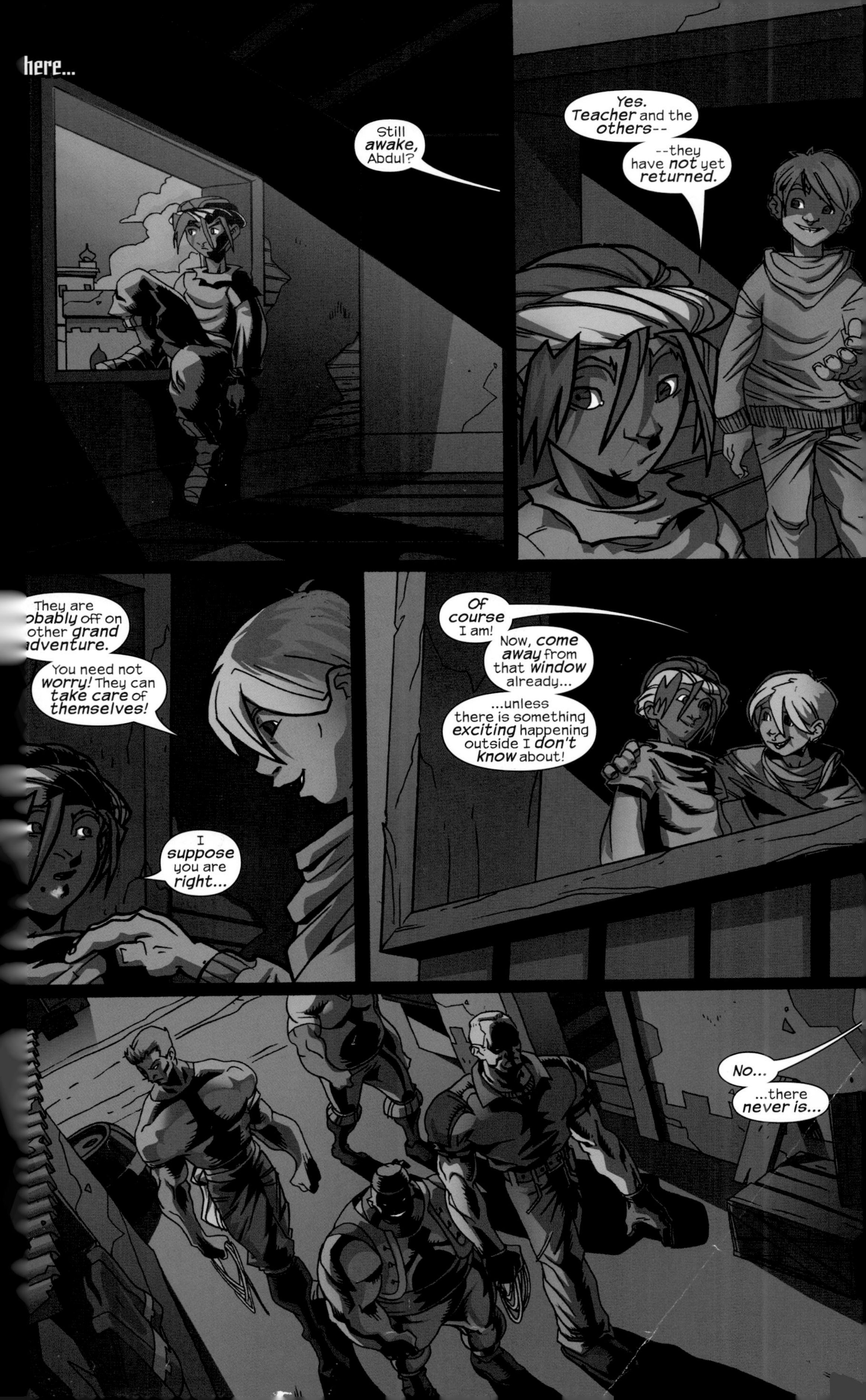
here...
Still awake, Abdul?
Yes. Teacher and the others--
--they have not yet returned.
They are obably off on other grand adventure.
You need not worry! They can take care of themselves!
I suppose you are right...
Of course I am!
Now, come away from that window already...
...unless there is something exciting happening outside I don't know about!
No...
...there never is...

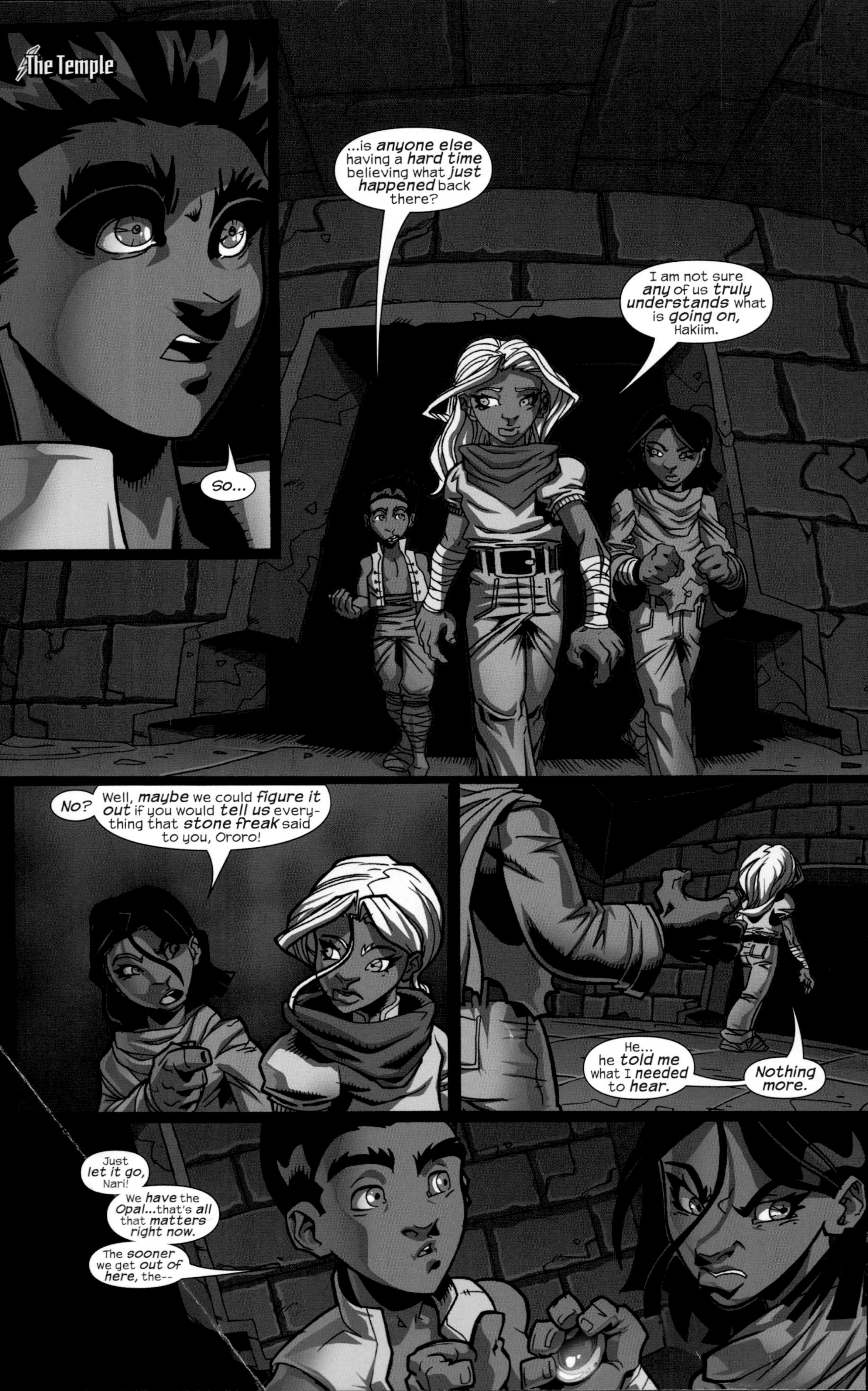
The Temple
So...
...is anyone else having a hard time believing what just happened back there?
I am not sure any of us truly understands what is going on, Hakiim.
No?
Well, maybe we could figure it out if you would tell us everything that stone freak said to you, Ororo!
He... he told me what I needed to hear.
Nothing more.
Just let it go, Nari!
We have the Opal...that's all that matters right now.
The sooner we get out of here, the--

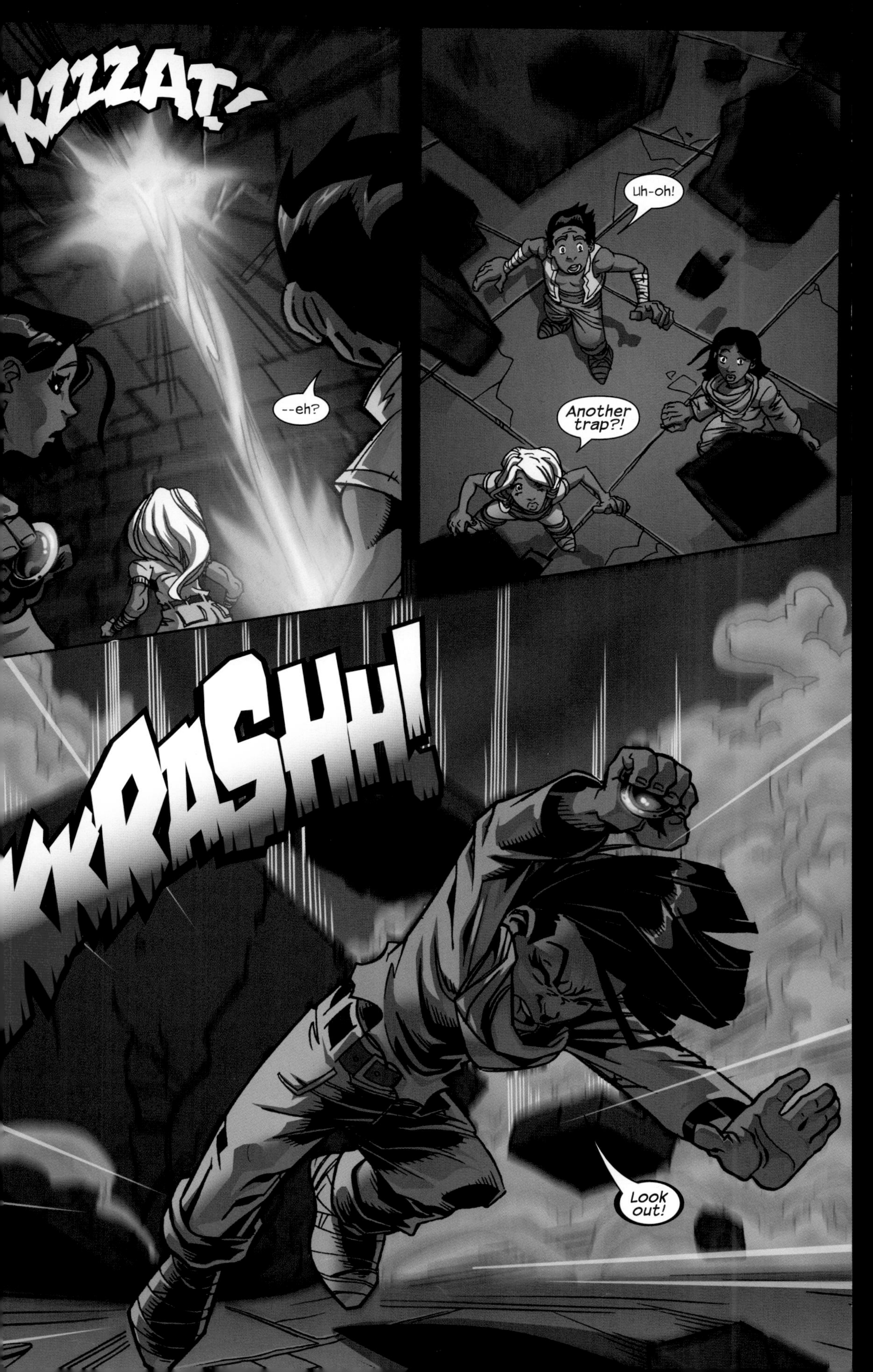
KZZZAT!
--eh?
Uh-oh!
Another trap?!
KRASHH!
Look out!

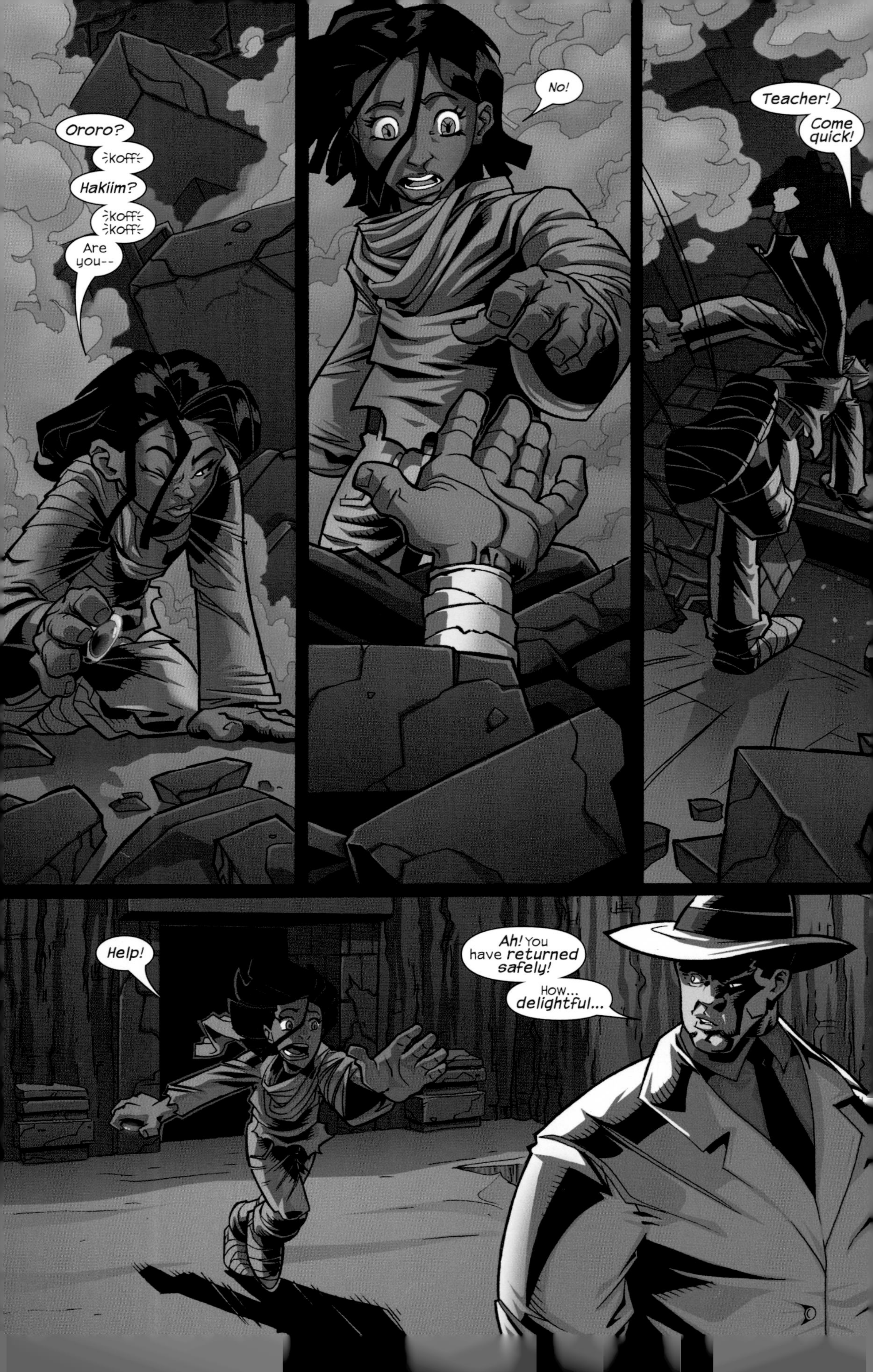
Ororo?
koff
Hakiim?
koff koff
Are you--
No!
Teacher!
Come quick!
Help!
Ah! You have returned safely!
How... delightful...

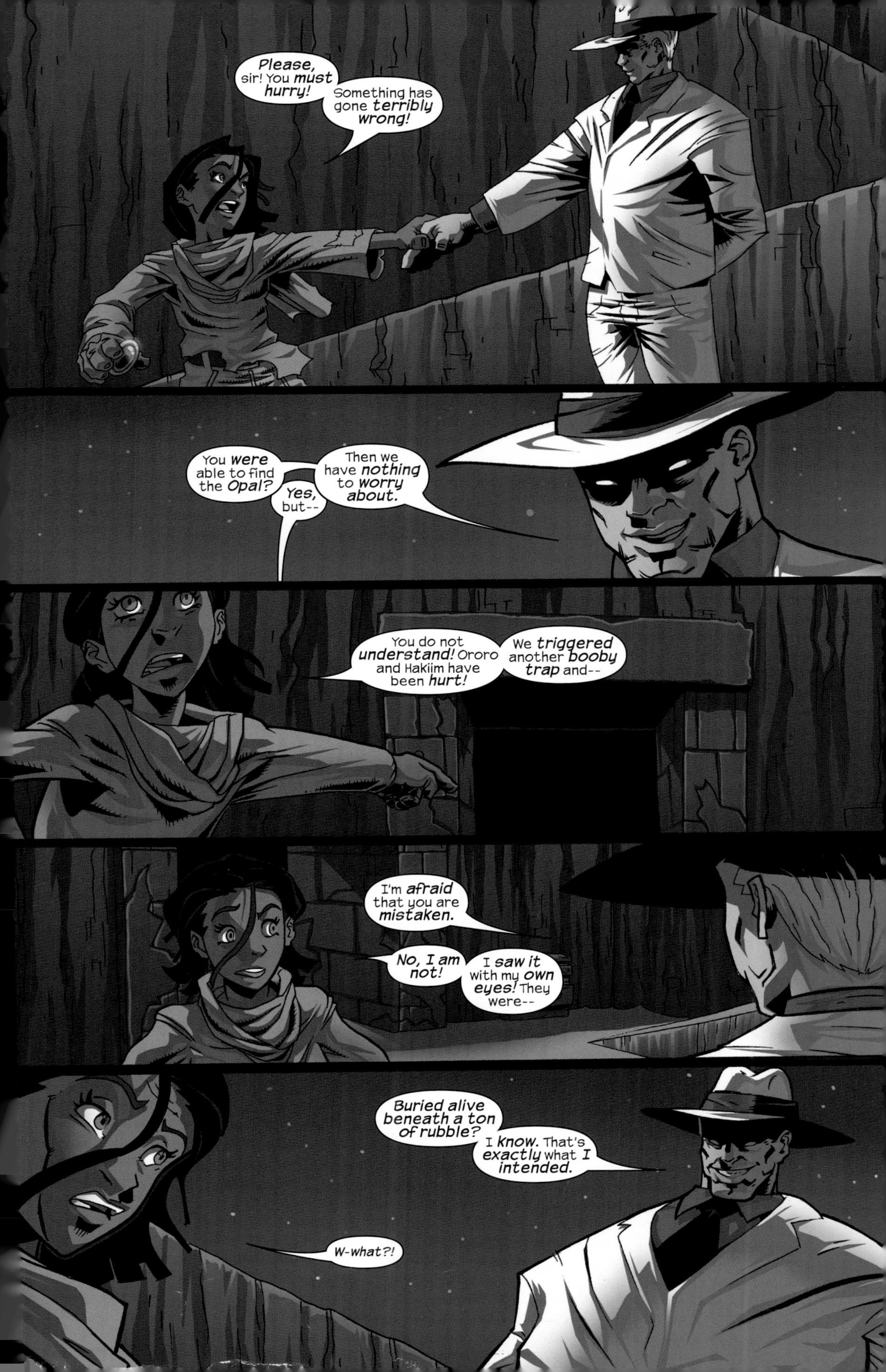
Please, sir! You must hurry!
Something has gone terribly wrong!
You were able to find the Opal?
Yes, but--
Then we have nothing to worry about.
You do not understand! Ororo and Hakiim have been hurt!
We triggered another booby trap and--
I'm afraid that you are mistaken.
No, I am not!
I saw it with my own eyes! They were--
Buried alive beneath a ton of rubble?
I know. That's exactly what I intended.
W-what?!

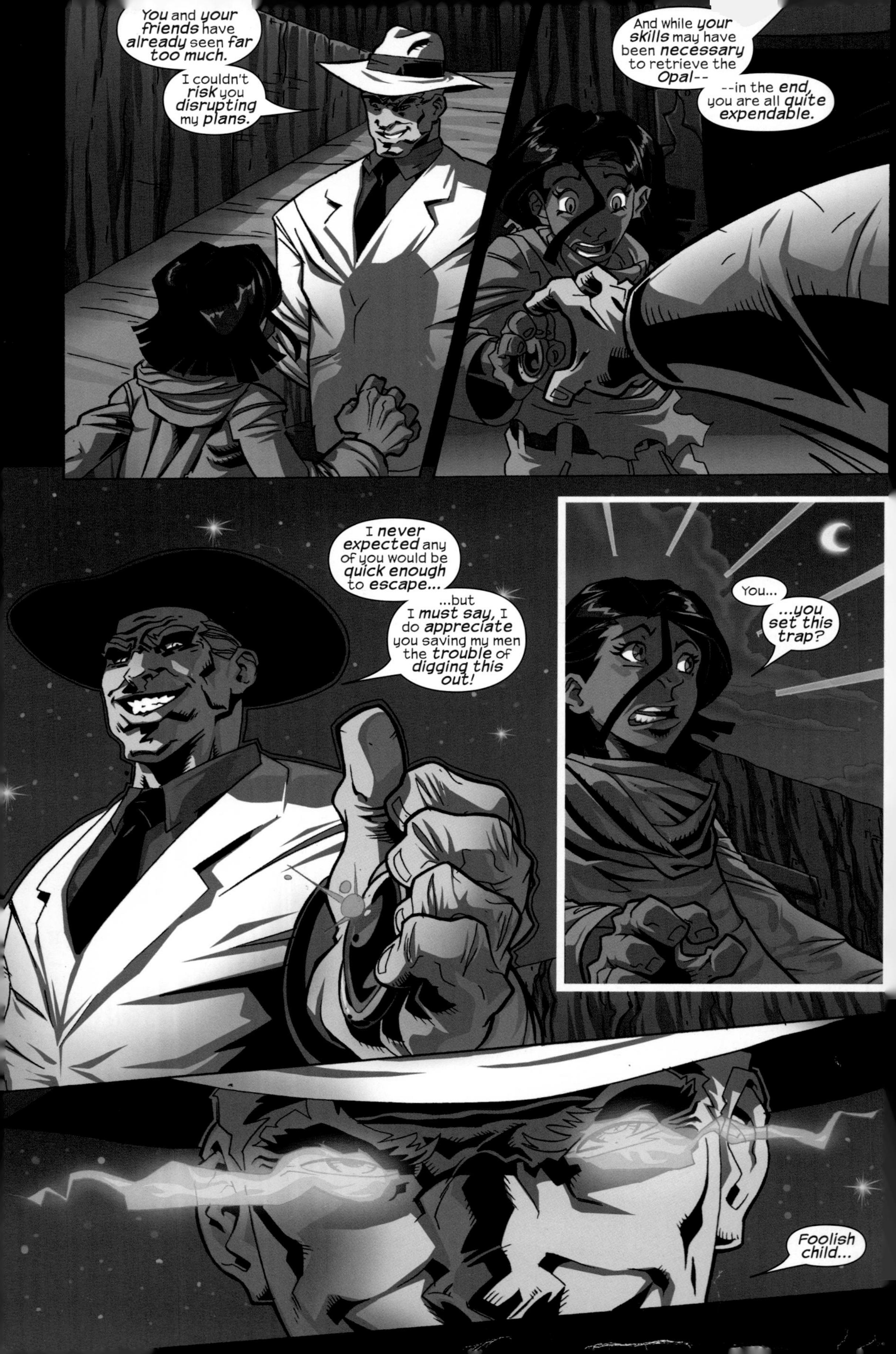
You and your friends have already seen far too much.
I couldn't risk you disrupting my plans.
And while your skills may have been necessary to retrieve the Opal--
--in the end, you are all quite expendable.
I never expected any of you would be quick enough to escape...
...but I must say, I do appreciate you saving my men the trouble of digging this out!
You...
...you set this trap?
Foolish child...

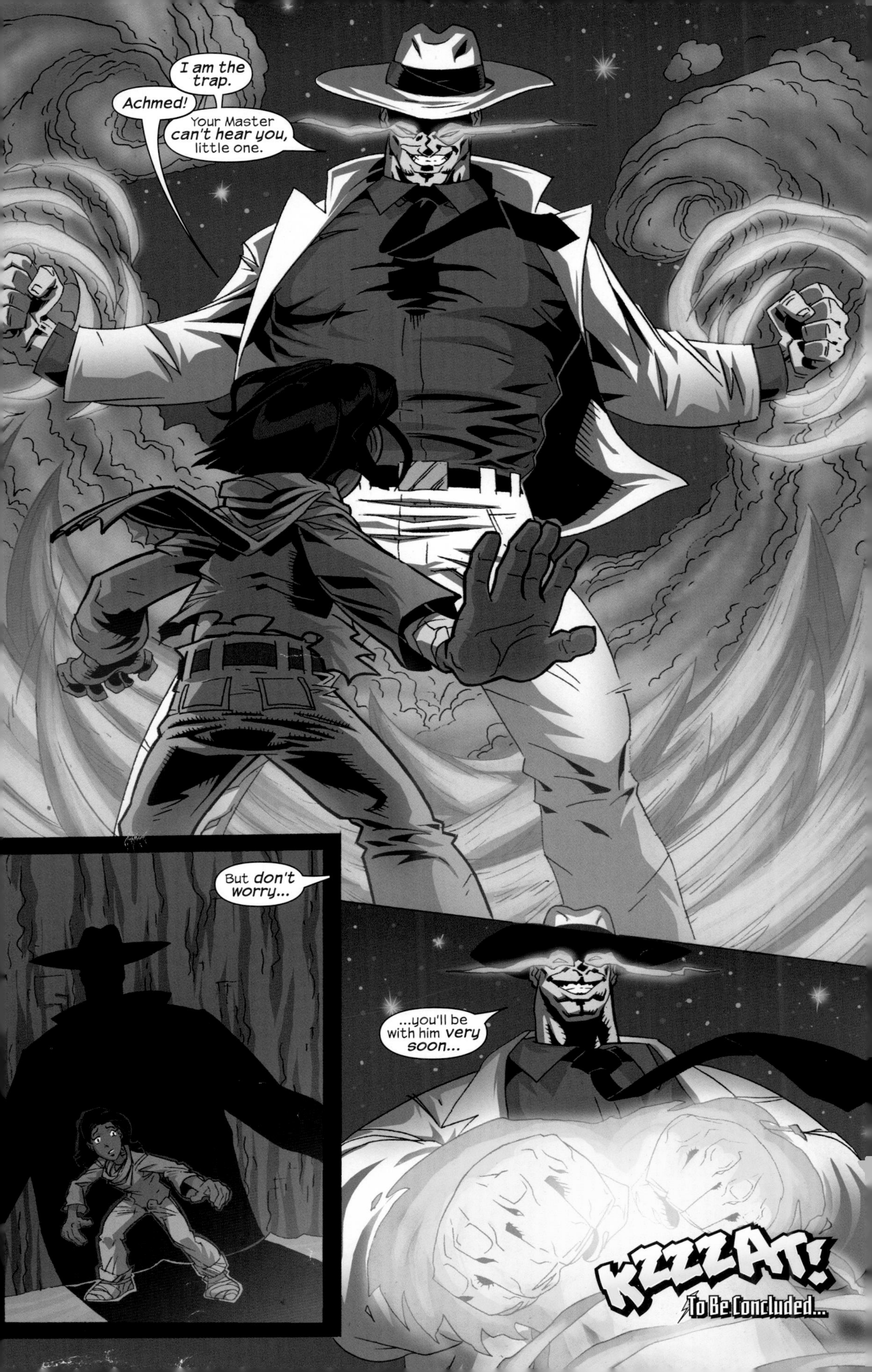

I am the trap.
Achmed!
Your Master can't hear you, little one.
But don't worry...
...you'll be with him very soon...
KZZZAT!
To Be Concluded...

visit us at www.abdopublishing.com

Reinforced library bound edition published in 2013 by Spotlight, a division of the ABDO Group, 8000 West 78th Street, Edina, Minnesota 55439. Spotlight produces high-quality reinforced library bound editions for schools and libraries. Published by agreement with Marvel Entertainment, LLC. The stories, characters, and incidents mentioned are entirely fictional. All rights reserved. Used under authorization.

Printed in the United States of America, North Mankato, Minnesota.
052012
092012
♻ This book contains at least 10% recycled materials.

marvelkids.com

TM & © 2012 Marvel & Subs.

Library of Congress Cataloging-in-Publication Data

Sumerak, Marc.
  Ororo : before the Storm / story by Marc Sumerak ; art by Carlo Barberi. -- Reinforced library bound ed.
     <v. 1-> cm. -- (Ororo)
  "Marvel."
  Summary: Long before she became the X-Man known as Storm, a young orphan named Ororo Munroe stalks the streets of Cairo, stealing under the tutelage of Achmed El-Gibar and yearning for the greatness her mother knew she would find.
   ISBN 978-1-61479-024-2 (part 1) -- ISBN 978-1-61479-025-9 (part 2) -- ISBN 978-1-61479-026-6 (part 3) -- ISBN 978-1-61479-027-3 (part 4)
  1. Graphic novels. [1. Graphic novels. 2. Superheroes--Fiction. 3. Orphans--Fiction. 4. Robbers and outlaws--Fiction. 5. Cairo (Egypt)--Fiction. 6. Egypt--Fiction.] I. Barberi, Carlo, ill. II. Title.
  PZ7.7.S86Oro 2012
  741.5'973--dc23
                              2012000932
  ISBN 978-1-61479-026-6 (reinforced library edition)

All Spotlight books are reinforced library binding
and manufactured in the United States of America.